EYE OF THE BEHOLDER

EMMA JAY

CHAPTER 1

Grayson Adams put the final touch on the painting and sat back in his chair, lifting his hand to his jaw as he considered the product. The details were as perfect as he could make them, but the painting lacked anything…special.

"I need a new muse," he murmured. Something different, unique. A virgin, maybe, a girl raised in the strictures of society. The forbidden aspect such a thing would generate would infuse passion in his work again.

His current model flipped her skirts down and sat up. "So you want a poke now?"

He moved his chair back, needing distance from her, from the painting, which didn't please him as it should. He could understand her misconception. He'd painted her in the most intimate of poses, had touched her body as he arranged her, but the gestures stirred no reaction in him. Perhaps that was why her painting didn't.

"Not this time," he said.

She pouted and rested her fists on her hips. "You gave the other girls a poke. They spoke well of your attributes."

He reached into his pocket and drew out the silver coins, adding a few extra to the agree-upon amount. He dropped them into the palm the girl opened reflexively.

"Thank you for your time. My man will see you out."

Once she was gone, he turned the painting to the wall. Perhaps he'd like it better once he had some distance.

No one in society realized the man dancing with their virginal daughters made his living painting women in seductive, intimate poses, spent his days in a garret with naked women who smelled of sex. He moved among the elite, finding pleasure in his secret. Grayson Adams, youngest son of the Baron of Cricksham, made a fortune selling erotic art that outstripped his oldest brother's inheritance.

And wondering how he could seduce one of them into modeling for him.

Now, with his new idea, the idea to paint a virgin, his desire to socialize increased. He rose, stretched, and went upstairs to dress for the evening.

SARAH DUSENBERRY EDGED CLOSER to the wall, a glass of lemonade in hand, and watched the dancers whirl across the floor in clouds of pastel. The musicians to her left and the hum of conversation to her right overwhelmed her senses, and she longed to slip out the French doors onto the patio. But the doors were some distance down the wall and moving toward them put her at risk of conversation with other guests. The possibility held no appeal.

Her mother insisted she attend these events, and as Sarah grew older, her mother grew more manic. Sarah was one-and-twenty, and now attended two balls a week. She was irritated and exhausted—and no match for the sixteen-year-old girls spinning across the floor on the arms of the most eligible bachelors London had to offer.

Her mother's target wasn't a man with money, but a man with a name. Sarah had a large dowry, though not quite large enough to tempt the titles her mother craved. Not large enough to account for her wild hair, long nose and tart tongue, which she wielded in a desire to keep her independence.

Murmurs ran through the crowd and Sarah followed their gazes to the door.

Her breath arrested in her throat. Grayson Adams stood in the doorway, surveying the group before him.

The Rebellious Baron, they called him, though that was his father's title, and he was unlikely to inherit, since his much-older brother had three sons himself. Still, Sarah admired no one in society more. In addition to being handsome—though not fashionably so with his broad shoulders and broad features, his hair longer than dictated, and allowed to curl, his sideburns trimmed, his jaw perpetually unshaven—he was the man who made these balls endurable, though of course he didn't attend as many as she. That was the only joy she took as she prepared herself each evening—the anticipation of seeing him.

She'd never spoken to him and he never stayed long, but she thrilled in his presence as long as he was in attendance.

His appearance wasn't the only thing that made him stand out. No, rumor had it that he was in trade, and had already made more money than his brother's inheritance was worth. That scandalized most of the young women and their mothers, but intrigued Sarah. What did he do, exactly? And how did he have the nerve to buck convention to do it?

He turned and met her gaze. Her heart tripped when he cocked his head and smiled before stepping into the room.

She watched as he greeted other guests, though she was aware of other young women giving him a wide berth. He was aware, as well. Before she realized what she was doing, she'd moved from the wall into his path.

She stopped some distance away. They had not been properly introduced, and she respected society's rules enough to wait. Also, he was an intimidating man, at least twelve years her senior, and worldly.

Her mother appeared at her side. "Is there someone here you'd like to meet?"

Sarah turned to her mother, who must have been paying close attention to notice. Her mother would never accept Grayson Adams. Even if he was the youngest son of a duke, the rumors of him being in trade would have her mother in fits.

"No, Mother." But her gaze followed Grayson.

Her mother noticed and drew herself up. "I'm not feeling quite the thing. Would you like to go?"

Any other time, Sarah would have jumped at the chance to leave. Why did her mother wait until Grayson had arrived? Did she suspect Sarah's improper attraction?

She looked from Grayson to her mother and nodded resignedly. One day she'd have the courage to do something she wanted.

Today was not that day.

SARAH DIDN'T SLEEP WELL after a dream of being swept around the room in Grayson Adams's arms, only to have him turn her over for a younger woman with a larger fortune, so she was at the dining room table before the servants had finished cooking breakfast. The travel periodical she subscribed to had arrived, however. Just as well, she didn't want her mother to see it, and she could enjoy it over a leisurely breakfast.

Her mother didn't understand her desire to see other places. Well, maybe it wasn't a desire so much as a longing, since she would likely never travel out of England. Still, she liked indulging the fantasies.

She was nibbling on a piece of toast when an advertisement caught her eye.

"Artist model?" she read aloud. No experience necessary, three hours a day for a week. That would be something daring, wouldn't it? He wouldn't have to know who she was, that she was in society, and whatever money she earned would be hers. If she was brave enough to do this, perhaps she could find the courage to travel.

She heard her mother on the stairs and quickly tucked the paper beneath the folds of her skirt. Her pulse pounded in excitement. What did an artist model do? Sit still for long periods, no doubt. What else? Did the artist talk? Had he been to many places? Perhaps she could speak to him of her longing to travel.

The advertisement didn't say what time to call. Were artists late risers? She made a note to visit just after noon. She would tell her mother she was shopping, and take her maid Lily with her.

A plan in mind, she greeted her mother with a smile.

Her mother appeared taken aback by the welcome, and regarded her warily as she moved to the sideboard to serve her own breakfast, toast and tea, a far cry from Sarah's more ambitious meal.

"You look rather like the cat with the canary," her mother remarked, sitting beside her.

"I've just decided I must have new gloves like Miss Winstead had last night," Sarah lied smoothly. "Lily and I will go out after lunch to see if I can procure a pair."

"Perhaps you might call on Miss Winstead," her mother said hopefully. "And she can direct you where to go. Perhaps she'd even accompany you."

As much as her mother wanted her to find a husband, she also wanted Sarah to find a friend. Miss Winstead was sadly very far down the list of the young women Sarah could tolerate, and she was only seventeen years old.

But to placate her mother, she agreed, too happy with

her decision to agitate her mother. Again, her mother gave her an odd look, so Sarah kissed her cheek and bounded up the stairs.

SARAH STOOD in front of the Bloomsbury address in the advertisement, not at all what she expected as an artist's loft. She tugged at the hem of her bodice, squared her shoulders, and marched up the steps to rap sharply at the door. She hoped she had the right address.

Behind her, Lily shifted her weight from one foot to the other. Sarah gave her an impatient wave to stop as she heard steps behind the door.

A butler swung the door open and Sarah stopped herself from taking a step back in surprise. Did artists have butlers?

"I'm here about the advertisement," she stammered, and pulled the paper out of her reticule.

The tall man, perhaps fifteen years her senior, raised his eyebrows as his gaze traveled up and down her dress.

Had she chosen wrong? She'd debated all morning over what to wear, finally choosing her best walking outfit. She'd presumed once she met with the artist, he would instruct her on what to wear. She stopped herself from touching her hair under her hat, a nervous habit.

"Am I in the right place?" she asked when the butler didn't respond.

"The right place, but I very much doubt you fit the specifications. Wait here."

He closed the door in her face, startling her, and she exchanged a glance with Lily.

"We don't belong here," Lily said quickly, her voice low as she reached for Sarah's arm. "Let's go before he comes back."

"I admit he's a little rude, but I've come this far. I'm not leaving now." Because she wouldn't have the courage to return.

So she stood on the front step and waited.

* * *

"WHAT IS IT?" Grayson grumbled when Dominic shoved back the drapes of his bedchamber. He'd been home a few hours, having spent the wee hours entertaining himself in a club playing cards with his friend John.

"Your advertisement has yielded a response."

"Good. Make an appointment."

"She is here."

"She's here?" Grayson opened one eye to look at Dominic. "Why would she be here?"

"She appears to be a well-born young lady."

"What would such a creature be doing responding to an advertisement for an artist's model?" he asked, rolling out of bed and rubbing his hands over his face. "What makes you think she is?"

"She's dressed buttoned to here," Dominic motioned to his chin, "and she brought her lady's maid with her."

"She did what?" He moved to the window and looked

down at the street, where he could only see the tops of the two women's heads.

"Who did you expect the advertisement would draw?" Dominic moved to Grayson's wardrobe.

"Not a young woman on her own. A merchant's daughter, perhaps, someone who needs the money."

"Perhaps this one does. Just because she comes from society doesn't mean she has money." He turned to Grayson, presenting a freshly pressed shirt and pants. "Shall I bring her in, or send her away?"

"Is she comely?"

"I'm not sure why that matters, since you don't paint their faces and it's hard to tell through all those petticoats if that particular attribute is attractive, but she's young and—tall."

Grayson stopped mid-reach. "So not pretty."

"I believe one would call her horse-faced." He tapped his nose.

Grayson grimaced and shrugged out of his sleep shirt and into his shirt. "She's here. Send her to the studio, alone. I don't want her maid in there." He shook his head. A model who was so conscious of conventions she didn't leave home without her maid would not be one who would part her legs for his paintbrush.

But he had to admire one who would have the courage to come here.

Dominic left and Grayson finished dressing on his own, suddenly anxious to meet this woman.

He slipped down the stairs to watch Dominic escort

the young woman, who had removed her hat, into the studio. And he drew back sharply.

He knew her. The young woman from the ball last night, the woman who had watched him so closely, as if she knew his secret.

And if he met with her, she would. He should call for Dominic to send her away, but damned if he wasn't intrigued. Once Dominic closed the door behind her, Grayson beckoned him.

"Light candles in the room, all around her."

Dominic's brow furrowed. Grayson drew to his full height. He should truly think about getting a manservant who didn't question him, but he'd grown rather attached to Dominic.

"The young lady has seen me in society."

Dominic's eyes widened and he turned back toward the studio door. "I'll send her on her way."

"No, don't."

Again Dominic delivered a questioning look.

"I'll stay to the shadows. I want to know what she's about."

"You risk too much," Dominic warned.

"I know what I risk. Do as I say."

Reluctantly, Dominic turned to do his bidding. Grayson waited on the landing until his manservant left the studio, then approached the door, taking a deep breath before he turned the handle.

She stood in the center of the room, her hat dangling from ribbons that she worked nervously through her hands. Her creamy skin was rendered soft by the candlelight, and her corkscrew curls cast lacy shadows on her face. Her plush lips parted in surprise when she heard the door, and her dark eyes reflected the flames around her.

"You are Monsieur Cresson?"

The French name he'd signed his paintings with sounded elegant from her lips. He savored it a moment before he realized she might know his voice. He came up with the only accent he could think of.

"Yes, my dear," he said in a heavy Italian cadence. "You are here to pose for me?"

Confusion creased her smooth brow a moment. "I —yes."

Unable to remain still, he crossed the room, careful to stay in the shadows. She followed his movement, eyes squinted as she tried to see him.

"May I ask why such a fine young woman would want to be an artist's model?"

"I have no reason that makes sense, other than I want an adventure."

"An adventure." He could give her that. He cleared his throat, realizing he'd forgotten his accent. "What are you willing to do to find this adventure?"

She lifted her face, lovely in the candlelight. What had Dominic called her? Horse-faced? The man was blind.

"Whatever you ask of me."

His voice shook, as if he was the one taking the risk, when he said, "Take off everything but your chemise."

She drew in a breath, but before she let it out, her hands moved to the buttons of her bodice. In a matter of moments, she was standing before him, the candlelight that hid him revealing her, the outline of her lush curves through the nearly transparent fabric, the hint of peaked nipples, the dark triangle of hair between her thighs.

"Stockings and shoes as well." He already realized just painting her sex wasn't going to be enough. He already had a vision of her, the pose, could already see the painting in his mind's eye. He wished he could sketch faster, as she bent at the waist to roll down her stockings and slip off her shoe. No, not necessary for her to pose for that one. The picture was indelibly printed on his mind.

"Take down your hair, and sit on the bed there, on your right hip." Damn her for knowing who he was. He wanted the freedom to go to her, touch her, position her, any excuse to caress that white skin. "Curve your knees toward me, and draw up the hem of your chemise just above your knees. That's right. Now place your hands on the bed and tilt your head down. Christ, you have lovely hair."

Her head came up at that, and a self-mocking smile played at her lips. "My hair is the bane of my existence."

"It's stunning. Different."

"You must not be in society much. Different is not better."

"Different is always better." He pulled back into the shadows before he gave into the desire to touch the billowy cloud. "Draw it forward, just a bit, over your left shoulder. I want it shadowing half your face. I want the mystery of a woman just rising from her lover's bed, the satisfaction, the knowledge."

The creamy skin darkened. "I don't know about that."

"You don't need to know. Brace your hands in front of you on the mattress there."

Her movement caused the right strap of her chemise to fall down her arm, and she reached to correct it.

"No, leave it," he ordered, dragging his stool in front of his easel and grabbing a charcoal pencil.

He started with the curve of her hip first, traced an outline of her leg, then traveled back up to her shoulder and arms, sketching only the slightest detail. He wanted the expression on her face, the lowered lashes, the slightly curved lips. God. He was hard just looking at her face. How could that be?

He worked in silence, keeping an eye on her for signs of discomfort with the pose. He saw none, not yet, as he sketched madly to capture that expression. If he accomplished nothing else today, he would accomplish that.

Then he started on her hair.

"I'm not able to get your hair just right," he muttered.

"I told you, it's more troublesome than it's worth."

He grunted, smudged, tried again. "It's lovely. It's just —it swoops here and curls there. It's as if I have to draw each strand separately." He sat back, dropping the pencil onto the table. "Would you like to take a break?"

"May I?" Relief colored her voice.

"Yes, of course."

She straightened, rolling her shoulders, and the chemise slipped a bit further, below her nipple. She gasped and snatched at the strap.

"When we resume, I want the strap lower," he said, doing his best to sound professional in his fake Italian accent when he was so hard he couldn't think of anything besides tasting her sweet flesh, plunging into that sweet body. "I want to see your breast."

That sweet body turned a delicious shade of pink. "If you're sure."

Her willingness made him even harder, and when she resumed her pose a few minutes later, after imbibing some tea delivered by Dominic, her rosy peaked nipple thrust out of the top of her chemise.

"Gorgeous," he murmured.

"No one's ever said that about me before," she said, shyly.

"Then the people you associate with are fools."

"I won't deny that, but for different reasons."

"Your society here is different than mine. They value different things."

"So how is it you have a French name and an Italian accent?"

"French father, Italian mother, raised in Italy."

"I've always wanted to visit Italy. Where did you live?"

"Florence." At least he'd visited there on his Grand Tour. He could speak of it with some knowledge.

She sighed. "The home of Michelangelo's David. Something I've longed to see."

"You are impressed with the male form?" he asked, a hint of humor in his voice.

Pink tinted her skin again. "With art. With the ability to create something where nothing was before. How could you leave such a place and come to live here?"

"Money is much better, and there are not so many artists as there are in Florence."

"I suppose I can see that."

"It's best to be unique."

"Not in England. Not for a woman."

"You sound unhappy with your lot."

"I'm not. I'm resigned to being a spinster, but I don't want my life limited to sewing parties and country house parties. And I dislike being pitied immensely."

"I shall make a note never to pity you," he said with a smile. He sat back in his chair. "I think that will do for today."

"May I see it?" She sat up but didn't immediately move to cover herself.

"Not yet. When it is done. Perhaps in a day or two. Can you return tomorrow?" After this pose, he already had two others in mind. Would she stay interested long enough?

At last she tugged her strap into place. "I will make a point of it."

"I'll pay you once the portrait is complete."

She looked up, blinking, as if she had forgotten about that. "Of course."

He moved toward the door to give her privacy to dress, something he'd never thought to do before. "I shall see you at the same time tomorrow?"

"I'll be here."

CHAPTER 2

Grayson tugged at his sleeves and looked into Lady Downing's stunned expression. He rarely attended balls two nights in a row, but his model had mentioned she would be here tonight, and he wanted to know her properly. He was drawn to her, dangerously so.

"You would…like to be introduced?"

He'd never requested an introduction to a young lady, though several had been thrust upon him. "I would. To Miss Dusenberry."

"Miss Dusenberry? I'm sure she's almost on the shelf. Surely you'd prefer a younger miss, who might be more biddable."

"I'm not looking to break a horse, ma'am, just to dance."

The older woman's eyes widened at his tone. "I'm just saying that Miss Dusenberry is known for her…strong opinions."

"Does she enjoy dancing?" Grayson pressed.

Lady Downing narrowed her gaze as if attempting to discern his purpose, then motioned for him to follow her.

Miss Dusenberry's lovely hair was piled in an unflattering style on top of her head,pulled tightly from her face as if that would disguise her curls, and the pink gown did nothing to accent that creamy skin. No, she needed jewel tones to stand out, not to blend in with all the young misses present.

She turned with wide eyes when Lady Downing took her arm.

"Miss Dusenberry, may I present Mister Grayson Adams?"

The pretty plump lips parted in surprise when she looked up at Grayson and for a moment he thought she might recognize him. But no, it was something else. He bowed deeply, showing more respect than her station warranted. She dipped into a curtsy and lifted her gaze.

"May I reserve a dance this evening, or are you spoken for?" he asked smoothly.

"I'm sorry. What?" Confusion darkened her eyes.

"Would you care to dance?"

Her forehead creased, and his body reacted as he remembered the expression from earlier.

"Miss Dusenberry?" prompted Lady Downing.

"Yes. Yes, I'd be honored."

He bowed again, then moved away with Lady Downing, leaving Sarah puzzling.

"Was that Grayson Adams?" her mother demanded, appearing at her side in an instant.

Sarah startled but didn't turn. Instead she watched Grayson walk away, nodding briefly to other guests, not looking back.

"Sarah!" her mother said sharply to draw her attention.

"It was."

"What did he want? An introduction?"

"And a dance."

"Grayson Adams doesn't dance with anyone," her mother's friend Mrs. Servin remarked, her own gaze following his departure. "It's often remarked upon, and we wonder why he bothers to come to the balls at all."

"What did you do to draw his attention?" her mother asked sharply.

"I have no idea," Sarah said, unwilling to allow her mother's disapproval to dim her excitement. She had to think of something to say as they danced or he would think her an utter fool. Already she had stumbled over his invitation to dance.

"We're aiming higher than a baron's younger son."

Sarah wanted to say something about beggars not being choosers, but she didn't want to engage her mother in a debate, not when she was thrilling over being singled out by the Rebellious Baron.

Not when she needed to be thinking about how to not act a fool in front of him.

He came to claim her for the dance a few moments later, after she'd replayed the proper steps in her head. Goodness, she didn't know why she was so anxious.

The attention they garnered when he took her arm to lead her onto the floor didn't help, either.

"Is it really so unusual for you to dance?" she asked as he turned her toward him in the formation.

"It's been awhile since I was moved to do so."

She bit the inside of her lip to stop herself from asking what moved him to do so now, but that might be perceived as pursuing a compliment and she didn't want him to find her so self-absorbed. The way he watched her throughout the dance was unnerving. And when he touched her, it wasn't quite proper, his fingertips brushing the skin of her arm above her glove. Her gaze lifted to his in alarm, but his was steady. Did he expect her to protest? Should she?

Instead, she hoped he'd do it again. And because of that, she struggled for conversation.

"If you do not care to dance, why do you attend balls?" she asked.

"There are more pleasures to be gained than on the dance floor."

"I've not found any."

Her words surprised a smile from him. "You're not a man."

She angled her head to look up at him. "What pleasures can a man find here that a woman cannot?"

His eyebrows lifted and a flush crept up her throat at her provocative question. "Aside from watching the lovely young ladies in their finery," he said, lowering his head toward hers so that his breath coasted warm over her throat, "there are card games, and smoking rooms, and other socialization."

"Which of those draws you?"

"I enjoy a friendly hand of cards and decent cigar." But his gaze traveled down the front of her gown, heating her skin, making her aware of her body as she hadn't since she went to the artist. Or perhaps she was aware because she went to the artist. "And you? Why do you come?"

She widened her eyes in mock censure that he would not know. "Why, I'm searching for a husband, of course."

His laugh drew the attention of all on the dance floor, and even the musicians stumbled for a moment before picking up the rhythm again. "What would you want one of those? They merely get in the way."

"Not as much as a mother, I imagine."

He laughed again, eyes crinkling in the corners as he looked down at her. "I suppose not, if you find the right one. The problem would be, one you would want to leave you alone would not be one you'd want on your wedding night."

His shocking words froze her for a moment, but his hand on her waist urged her into movement again.

"Perhaps you are not aware that such a topic is off-limits for unmarried women."

The eyebrows lifted again. "Unmarried women, in my experience, know much more about the wedding night than they care to let on. And look forward to it more than they want their husbands to know."

Why was he speaking to her so? Did her newfound awareness of her body show in her face? In her move-ments? Was she a loose woman now because she'd shown her breast to a painter?

The urge to flee, to inspect her face in the mirror for a

telltale sign was strong, but would draw attention to them. Would this song never end?

When it did, would Grayson Adams ask her to dance again?

Finally the song drew to a close, and Grayson stepped back, bowing deeply. "I regret that I have other commitments tonight, but now we are introduced. I shall see you again."

And without escorting her from the floor, he disappeared into the crowd.

"THE MASTER INSISTS you wear a blindfold today." The artist's man proffered the length of black cloth when she arrived at the townhouse the following afternoon.

Sarah stared at it. Why would he wish her blindfolded? Was it part of the art? Or did she know the man? She didn't know anyone from Italy, but perhaps she'd seen him in society.

She took the blindfold and tied it around her head, adjusting the fabric over her eyes. Suddenly she felt even more daring, as if hiding her eyes hid her inhibitions as well. She heard the door open, then close, and she was alone. Her fingers hovered above the buttons of her dress. She hadn't been told to undress, but she would certainly feel more comfortable disrobing alone than in front of Monsieur Cresson.

She had just folded her dress over her arm when the

door opened and she heard him enter. She turned toward the door, resisting the urge to cover herself.

"Let me take that for you," he said, after a moment of silence, then lifted the dress from her. "Do you mind the blindfold?"

"No." She didn't want to admit the idea excited her.

"Good." He cleared his throat. "I have a few more details I want to address on yesterday's pose, and I'd like to begin another."

"Another? So soon?" She thought portraits took ages. And she certainly didn't think she'd perform more than one pose.

"I don't need you here for the painting," he said. "I have you in my mind. And you inspire me. Take your hair down."

His words sent a thrill through her and she reached up to remove the pins. Her curls tumbled against her suddenly-sensitized skin. Then she sensed him closer, smelled his spicy scent. He closed his hands over her shoulders and eased her backwards onto the bed where she'd been yesterday.

She tried to remember the pose but he reached to bend her knees toward him, sliding his hand up her thigh to adjust the hem of her chemise. Heat sizzled through her, along her leg to the place between her legs, and her breasts tightened. Her breath caught in her throat and she shivered, waiting for his touch on her hip, or where her body began to burn and crave. What she craved, she didn't know.

Then he moved away and her body ached for him to return.

He didn't speak, so she didn't.

"Your coloring is lovely," he murmured finally, and she jolted at the sudden sound when the only sound had been pencil to paper. "You should wear strong colors. Jewel tones. Reds, blues, greens. Pastels don't do justice to your skin."

Pastels? But she wore a dark blue striped day dress. What made him think of pastels? Unless he had seen her at a ball, where all the young unmarried women wore pastels.

"It's the fashion," she said.

"It's not imperative to be in fashion. In fact, I'd think a young woman who's doing what you're doing would not care about what's in fashion."

"I don't but my mother does. It's simpler to make her happy."

"And if she discovers what you're doing here?"

"I'm taking great care that she not find out."

"So why do you do it?"

She heard him shift, set something aside. The canvas, maybe. "I told you. I want adventure."

"I'm ready for a new pose," he said long silent moments later. "Sit on your backside and lean back with your elbows behind you." He waited until she complied. "Now, draw your legs up, your knees bent."

He moved close again, and closed his hand over her bare knee, drawing her legs apart, just a bit, so she felt a breeze on her most private parts. She drew in a sharp breath when he pushed up the hem of her chemise, and she suddenly felt naked. But she didn't move as he arranged the fabric, then removed his touch and stepped back.

She wanted his touch again, the brush of his rough fingertips against her untouched skin. Then he moved close, his fingers closing around her ankle and easing her legs open a little more.

The instinct to close her knees was overwhelming, but she fought it, especially when she heard his breathing change. No one had seen her most intimate part, not even herself, and this man she didn't know was looking at it. She felt her flesh heat, swell, grow wet. A flush traveled over her skin.

"Lovely," he said finally, and the air cooled when he stepped away. "Now, I want you to let your head fall back."

The sound of the easel being dragged to a new position echoed through the room. She did as he asked, and felt a twinge in her neck.

"I'm not certain I can hold this pose."

"I'll get you some pillows, but you must not relax your arms." He spoke from near her feet.

The position alarmed her. He was painting her most intimate area? She couldn't work the courage to ask, and didn't know what to call it in any case. Certainly she didn't want to ask him. He went to the door and summoned his man, and she jolted. She didn't want the man to see her in this position.

"No, don't move," Monsieur Cresson said sharply. "He won't enter."

In a matter of moments, the door opened, and Monsieur Cresson moved to her head, propping pillows behind her head. Then he moved silently to the end of the bed and began to draw.

All she could think about was her exposed sex and how warm the realization made her, how restless. Now she no longer wanted to close her legs but spread them wider. This unknown hunger began to consume her, and her breathing grew heavier.

Her scent carried through the air. Grayson's trousers became tight as he became aware of Sarah's arousal. His cock responded with enthusiasm, and while he was trying to catch the curve of her chin just so, his gaze traveled again and again to her sweet sex, with its dark curls growing damp with her arousal. Her body was still, but he could sense her restlessness, understood it. He wanted to touch her so badly, wanted to thrust his fingers into her tight sheath, draw that wetness up over her swelling flesh, wanted to hear her moan in a pleasure she had never known before. An idea for another pose came to him, and he hoped she'd be willing to try it.

First he had to finish this sketch, and to do so, he needed to concentrate. He couldn't as long as his cock strained against his fly. Perhaps if he eased himself, he could focus. The problem was, he wanted to ease himself right here.

He shoved back his chair. "You must be getting stiff. Get up, move around, and I'll be back in a moment."

"Where are you going?"

But he couldn't tell her, instead slipped out into the hall, and hurried up to his bedroom.

A virgin. What had he been thinking, bringing a virgin into his studio? He yanked down the flap of his trousers and drew out his erection, sighing in relief. If she was a whore, he could take his release with her, perhaps in her mouth so that he wouldn't ruin the pose.

Sarah had a lovely mouth. As he closed his fist around his cock, he imagined those sweet full lips closing around him, her delicious little tongue darting out to taste the liquid that formed on the tip, to stroke around the head. In his mind, she'd know just what to do, though he imagined the real Sarah would never have thought such a thing possible.

Fantasy Sarah's mouth traveled down his shaft, taking more of his cock into the heat of her mouth, her tongue stroking, building on his pleasure, her mouth pulling on his cock with a delicious suction. His fist moved faster as he pumped against Fantasy Sarah's mouth, as his balls tightened, and he came across the sheets of his bed, the climax powerful for being masturbatory. He leaned against the bedpost for a moment as Fantasy Sarah dissolved.

Christ, what was wrong with him that he couldn't control his desires any more than that?

rayson tossed down his charcoal the following day and sat back, scrubbing his hand over his face.

"What is it?" Sarah asked, her head still tilted back in the pose.

There was something to be said for good girls. They did what they were told, no matter what.

"Not sure," he muttered. He'd captured the surrender of her, head back, revealing that fine chin, the smooth line of her throat. He'd sketched the hills of her breasts beneath the chemise, the thrust of her nipples. He was happy with the folds of the chemise above her sex, and happy with the depiction of her sex itself, dark, damp, mysterious. She wasn't as aroused as yesterday, but her tender flesh was swollen enough to give him a hint of pink. He was pleased with the bend of her legs and her feet.

"I have a thought," he said at last, and rose to fetch the pitcher of water from the nearby table. "This will be cold."

"What?" she asked, breathless, just as he poured a stream of water over her breasts, plastering her chemise to her, rendering it transparent.

She gasped and bowed upwards, her hair brushing against the front of his trousers, and yes, he was hard again. Especially when he looked down at her nipples, tight and dark beneath the fabric. He wanted to take each in his mouth, wanted to warm them, feel them against his tongue. He pushed the thought away and returned to his canvas to see the effect. Not quite what he wanted. He picked up the pitcher again, and with no warning, dribbled the water between her breasts to her navel, so the fabric clung to her from neck to pubis. He returned to the canvas and inspected his subject.

He was fully aroused now, but couldn't excuse himself, not when her chemise would dry soon, ruining the picture. He adjusted himself and sat before the easel again, sketching the defined curves of her breasts, the peaks of her nipples, the indentation of her navel. She was all but naked, and so beautiful.

"Monsieur Cresson," she chattered a few moments later. "I'm very cold."

He noticed then, the gooseflesh on her arms and legs. He shoved to his feet and strode to the door. "Dominic, we need more wood for the fire."

Dominic appeared in short order, and behind him, Grayson heard Sarah gasp.

"Do not move," he warned her. "He's only seeing to the

fire." But when Grayson turned back, he placed himself between her and Dominic, aware of the flush of embarrassment covering her skin. Dominic added wood to the fire and turned away, with only a glimpse at the canvas and a nod of approval.

When the door closed again, Grayson patted her foot —her very cold foot—and sat at the easel again.

"Don't be ashamed of your body, my dear. Men will be seeing this painting, you know."

"But they will not know it is me."

"True. I'm sorry. I didn't think. He kept his gaze averted in any case."

"Kind of him."

She resumed her pose with very little adjustment needed on his part, and he began to sketch again, capturing the fall of the fabric, the plushness of her body. A shame it had to be hidden so completely.

"Do you go to a ball tonight?" he asked to distract himself.

"A musicale. Doubly dull, I'm afraid."

"Do you perform?" The idea intrigued him.

"I do, but despise it."

"Tell me you are not shy."

Her laugh sent a warm sensation through him. "I am deathly shy."

"I would not have suspected." He nudged her foot with the end of his pencil. "Do you sing or play?"

"Both."

"Very accomplished, then."

"I did not say I do either well."

"I would enjoy hearing you sing."

"Oh, very unlikely without accompaniment and threats from my mother."

"So this you do, this you do for me, it is retribution against your mother?"

"Not at all. I love my mother and like to please her. I only wish her interests could be diverted elsewhere. It is clear I'll never marry."

"Why is it clear?"

"I'm very high on the shelf, Monsieur."

"That is ridiculous."

"Men want girls who are malleable. Younger women tend to be."

"Who told you what men want?"

That gave her pause. "My mother."

"Does she know well what men want?"

She laughed. "She believes so."

"What does your father say?"

"He died when I was eight."

"I'm sorry."

"He was a gambler. He was killed in a duel because he was accused of cheating at cards."

"So your mother has been alone? She never remarried?"

"She did. He died as well, of a heart attack, when I was twelve. She married again the following year."

Grayson paused. "So if she was able to marry three times, well past the age of malleability, why does she discount your chances?"

"She doesn't. I do. My mother is one who adapts to what men want. I do not."

"Perhaps you have not found the man who makes you want to."

"I don't believe he exists." She rolled her weight on her elbows a bit. "What do you look for in a wife? Do you think you can find a woman who will accept your form of art?"

"I'm a younger son. My brother has three sons of his own. It's not required that I marry."

"At least there is no stigma attached there."

"But certainly enough speculation."

"So you are in society, then?"

He cursed himself. Had she designed the question to discover his identity? "Now and then."

"Have we met?"

"Miss Dusenberry, I prize my privacy, as you can imagine. My two worlds must not meet." He set his pencil down, pleased that he'd captured her shape beneath the damp gown. "You may get dressed. I shall see you tomorrow."

"A MUSICALE?" Dominic asked skeptically. "On purpose?"

"She will be there. Singing, if she can be believed."

"Do you plan to court this young woman?"

"I'm not sure what I plan," Grayson said as he stepped out of the room and headed down the stairs.

She was just rising to perform when he slipped in the

back of the room. He heard the murmurs, saw the veiled glances in his direction as he chose a chair in the back, on the end. But the whispers had drawn Sarah's attention as well, and she widened her eyes to see him. Her hand fluttered near her throat, above a very fussy lace color on a pale yellow dress and appeared panicked as she sat behind the pianoforte. Her fingers flexed in a gesture he recognized as nerves.

He hadn't intended to make her nervous. He'd merely wanted to hear her sing. She lifted her gaze to his and he pointed to himself, then to the door, asking if she wanted him to leave. She gave a short shake of her head and let her fingers drop to the keyboard.

And she played. Passably, as she had claimed, and her voice joined the melody, again, passably. But he found her skill adorable and wondered what the hell was going through his head to be pursuing a debutante, even one as unique as Sarah Dusenberry.

He sat through four more young ladies' performances that made Sarah sound like a virtuoso. She returned to her seat and Grayson allowed himself to study her profile. Her upswept curls were not well-behaved, and escaped in wisps to tease her long white neck. She wore an ugly yellow gown, but it showed her lovely figure. Perhaps he could paint a real portrait of her, emphasizing those plush lips, those long eyelashes, that gorgeous skin.

At last the hostess rose and announced they'd have lemonade and games. Her own expression betrayed surprise when she saw Grayson in attendance. He nodded regally, as if he had every right to be here and hadn't just walked in uninvited.

He approached Sarah, who stood in the back of the room with a tiny cup of lemonade gripped in her hand. Her eyes were huge when he stopped beside her.

"Mr. Adams. I don't believe I've ever seen you at a musicale before."

"I don't often attend." In fact, he'd been to one, a dozen years ago. He'd presumed he'd suffered enough. "Your performance was lovely."

She waved a dismissive hand, her focus on the crowd—and the attention they were getting. "You clearly haven't attended many."

"My feeling was that your heart wasn't in your performance, that it's something you do because you feel you need to, not because you want to."

"Your instincts could be right."

"What do you enjoy doing? Do you enjoy riding?"

"I have no great passion for it." But a playful light shone in her eyes.

The devil prodded him to do it, just to see her reaction. Would she demur or would she cancel her sitting? "Would you care to go riding tomorrow afternoon?"

Something flared in her eyes, and he felt guilty, just for a moment, for making her choose.

"I'm afraid I have an appointment."

"The following day, then."

The confusion that creased her brow echoed his own. Why was he so determined to spend time with her?

Weren't the hours they spent while he was painting her enough?

"I believe I can arrange something," she said, her voice a little breathy.

He gave a short bow just as her mother approached. "I shall call for you then." He nodded to her mother, excused himself, and walked away.

* * *

SARAH WAS surprised when she walked into the studio the following day to see Monsieur Cresson wearing a domino and a hat. He usually came into the studio after she was here, and she was the one to wear the blindfold. His need to wear the disguise had her studying him more closely. His hair was hidden by the hat, and his eyes were down-turned, their shape distorted by the mask. His mouth was shadowed by dark stubble, his throat strong above the open collar of a white shirt. His shoulders were broad, waist narrow, legs long. She should know. She'd watched people enough in society, but none she knew had an Italian accent.

"We're trying a new pose today."

"But you have not finished the others."

"I'm doing the preliminary sketches now. I need to get the ideas on paper before I lose them."

"So I won't be needing a blindfold today?"

"Not at first. We're going to have a—lesson, you might say."

"A lesson?" Her fingers went to the buttons of her

bodice as they spoke. Had she ever expected she would be comfortable undressing in front of a man? "What kind of lesson?"

"Anatomy."

Tension ratcheted a little higher but it wasn't an unpleasant sensation. "Mine, I suppose."

"Have you ever touched yourself?" he asked, and her hands stilled, her gaze darting to his.

"I beg your pardon?"

He took a step closer and her breath caught in her throat. "I've been painting your sex, Sarah. Yesterday in particular, I know the idea excited you."

She took a step back, her legs bumping into the bed. "You were looking at me. Very intently. No one has ever seen that part of my body."

"Tell me how you felt when I was looking at you, Sarah."

"I was—warm. And I could feel my heart beat there. I felt like I was—perspiring there. I felt a need for something that I didn't understand."

"You were sexually aroused. Your body was preparing for a lover, softening, growing slicker." He took another step closer, unhooked her skirt and let it fall to the floor. His hands brushed her hips through the chemise, sending a shiver through her. "Sit on the edge."

Her nerves shimmered on the outside of her skin as he lifted her onto the bed and eased the hem of her chemise higher and higher along her thighs, until she felt the air on her sex. He bent, just a bit, to adjust the folds of the fabric, and his breath was warm on her leg. Again she felt the flesh between her legs heat and swell and grow moist. He eased her legs apart, opening them wider, so that each knee hooked over a corner of the bed. She wanted to cover herself with her hand at the same time she wanted him to look, to touch.

Goodness, what was wrong with her?

Then he had a mirror and placed it between her spread legs. He started to touch her, but she gasped, and he curled his fingers back.

"Do you see?"

She couldn't think, couldn't form words.

"Sarah. Do you see?"

"Yes."

"This." He pointed to a sliver of slick pink flesh on the glass. "This is the clitoris. This is the center of a woman's pleasure. If it's stroked, it can relieve the pressure you were experiencing, sending waves of enjoyment through you, leaving you satisfied. This." He pointed to a deeper fold. "This is where a man puts his cock, pushes deep until it is completely buried. It stretches the flesh, and for a virgin it's painful, but the pain passes and is replaced by pleasure as he moves his cock in and out."

Just his words, imagining his body doing that to hers, made her breathing shallow, her heart beat faster, until she could feel it in the very area where he pointed.

"This is your rose," he continued, moving down so that she had to shift to look. "I am sure you know the purpose. This can also be a pleasurable thing, if a man knows just what he is doing."

"Do you know what you're doing?" she asked, breathless, surprised by her own boldness.

He flicked his gaze to hers. Green eyes. Bright, surprised, light with humor. "I do."

She drew in a sharp breath as his finger moved along the mirror as if he was caressing her.

"Sometimes, a man will kiss a woman there, as he would kiss her mouth, and it will make her spend."

"Spend?"

"Reach completion, find pleasure."

"With his mouth? With a kiss?" She knew if he even breathed against her right now something wonderful would happen. She shifted her hips toward him, wanting to know where this alien sensation would lead.

"What I want you to do," he said, placing the mirror on the table behind him, and reaching for her hand, "is touch yourself."

Heat bloomed over her face. "I cannot."

"You didn't think you could pose for me, either. I want you to take these two fingers." He bent her fingers. "And touch your quim."

"My--?"

"Another word for your sex. The French call it la chatte. 'Little cat.'"

"I like it better. Seems less silly."

"Will you touch it?"

She held his gaze and moved her hand down, fingertips brushing over the curls. She gasped to find the flesh beneath soft and slick and so sensitive to the touch. Despite her awareness that Monsieur Cresson was watching her closely, his own breathing uneven, she stroked again, and again, the forbidden delight shooting through her body, the flesh swelling under her hand. The wetness coated her fingers and she pushed her hips toward her own touch, seeking the prize that seemed to be offered her.

"Stop," he said, his voice rough, and she realized he'd moved behind the easel. "Christ, I wish I could draw fast enough. What I want you to do now is put those fingers in your mouth."

She snapped her gaze to his. "What?"

"I want you to taste yourself, and I want you to hold that pose."

"I cannot do that! It's—indecent!"

He chuckled. "You sit before me touching your quim, my dear. Trust me."

Because she did, because her curiosity overwhelmed her, her desire overwhelmed her, she lifted her fingers to her lips and darted her tongue out to test. Salty, but not unpleasant. She took another hesitant taste. He groaned.

"Slide them into your mouth, just the tips, and close your lips around them."

She did, feeling dirty and excited all at once. Her quim throbbed, wanting her to pet it again, but Monsieur Cresson moved forward, adjusting her fingers and admonishing her to hold the pose, as her legs remained open, her sex hot with longing. She wanted to see what would happen if she continued to pet it, she wanted to know what it would feel like if he touched her, but she couldn't ask, couldn't do more than hold the pose until he gave her permission to stop.

"That's enough for today," he said, pushing back from his easel and rising.

"I want this feeling to end," she said, need overwhelming her sense of propriety. "Will you show me?"

He made a strangled sound. "You want me to pet your chatte?"

"I want to know what it feels like."

She watched him, saw the indecision flicker across his face, saw his gaze drop to her weeping, aching quim.

"You can do it. I can instruct you."

"I want you."

"I don't know if I have the reserves to resist you."

"You do. You do." Suddenly she wanted nothing as much as his hands on her body. Her breasts swelled, aching for his touch, her body throbbed for it. "Please, Monsieur. I must know."

Grayson couldn't resist, though he would rather hear his own name on her lips. He climbed on the bed behind her and drew her against his chest. The scent of her arousal filled the room, making him drunk with his own desire, a desire he couldn't unleash at the risk of losing control and taking her virginity.

She nestled against his chest, her bottom snug against his heavy cock. He resisted the urge to push against her, instead rested one hand on her waist and one on her thigh. Her breathing was frantic, her pulse raced, and he slid a hand to cup her breast as he lowered his lips to the curve of her throat. She trembled all over and gasped in delight, craning her head to offer him more white flesh. He dragged his lips and tongue along the line of her throat, nipping just below her ear as he pinched the tip of her breast between his fingers.

Slowly, his hand on her thigh slid up until his palm covered her mound. She bucked her hips against it, but he wanted to drag the sensation out. He stroked two fingers over the outer lips, wishing he was bold enough to put his own lips over them, and bring her to completion with his tongue. He wanted to thrust his tongue inside her opening, wanted to feel her push against his mouth. Instead he settled for her pushing against his hand, whimpers coming from her throat.

He dragged his fingertip in the lightest caress over her swollen clitoris, then dipped his finger against her opening to drag more wetness across her flesh.

"Please, there. Touch me there," she gasped. "I have to know."

Despite his own desire, he circled his fingertip over the nub, feeling her body tightened, hell, feeling his own body tighten as she wriggled against him.

And then she spent, her hips pushing against his hand, her breath escaping in wild cries, her juices coating his fingers. He continued his caress until she fell lax against his chest, breathing hard.

"Was wonderful," she managed at last, rolling her head against his shoulder to look up at him. "Something was missing, though."

"My cock inside you," he said, pressing his hips against her backside without thinking.

She rolled her bottom against him. "I feel it. May I see it?"

"No."

"Why not? You've seen my most intimate parts, and I want to understand the mystery."

"Because I do not have a great deal of self-control right now. I feel as restless as you did moments ago."

"I can help you find release."

The thought of her virgin hands—her virgin mouth—on his swollen cock only made him harder. He wanted to show her, but it wasn't the wisest choice.

And then she turned in his arms and slid her hand down the front of his trousers. He groaned and it was no longer his choice. She sat between his parted thighs and unfastened his trousers with some difficulty, her knuckles brushing the underside of his erection through the fabric. He clenched his teeth so he wouldn't spend in his pants like an untried youth.

"Let me," he said, finally pushing her hands away and parting the fabric, then bringing out his cock in his own fist.

She sat back. "It's larger than I expected."

"What every man wishes to hear," he said through gritted teeth.

"May I touch it?"

"When I spend, it's much messier than when you do," he advised. "Proceed with caution."

She glided delicate fingertips down his length, tracing veins, her nails lightly scraping his balls, which tightened in response. She explored the shape of them, then dragged her touch up to circle the head, flicking her finger over the drop of fluid and easing it over the skin.

"Hard and soft," she murmured, to herself.

"More hard than soft."

"How can I help you spend?" she asked, the last word not quite tripping off her tongue.

"Wrap your hand around me." He wanted her mouth on him so badly he couldn't think to tell her no. Instead he folded her hand around his width—and got harder—before guiding her movements, up and down. "This is the rhythm of sex. When you make love with your husband, he will slide in and out of you just like this."

She made a small sound that he interpreted as longing. "It's what was missing. The emptiness."

"Yes." She was watching him so closely, studying him, learning him.

"I want to kiss it. It's so very odd. May I kiss it?"

Yes! "No! I would—I--" He couldn't form words anymore, just imagined her lips brushing the sensitive head, her tongue touching his skin, and his cum spilled out, striping her thigh, pulsing over her hand.

Her gaze still on him, though her eyes were markedly wider, Sarah peeled her hand away and he climbed off the bed to fetch a cloth to clean her up. He could hardly send her back to her mother this way. But Christ, he was shaking.

"Is your curiosity quite satisfied?" he asked, managing not to sound breathless after his orgasm, tucking away his cock as she wiped herself clean.

She lifted those dark eyes to him. "More curious than

ever, I'm afraid. I can cancel my plans for tomorrow, return and you can show me more."

"I can show you no more," he said sharply. "You are a virgin, which is how you will leave me, each and every time."

"But I want to know."

"Then find a husband." He tossed his own cloth aside and strode toward the door. He very rarely walked away from temptation, but this time, he had no choice.

SARAH HURRIED DOWN THE STAIRS, tugging her gloves on, her heart stinging with Monsieur Cresson's rejection. Her good sense told her he was only looking out for her, but every other sense—her pride, her desire—ached with his words.

She placed her hand on the door leading into the kitchen, where Lily waited for her to complete each session. Sounds coming from the other side of the door urged her to proceed cautiously, and when she peeked through the crack in the door, she saw her hesitation was warranted.

Lily lay back on the table, knees raised, skirt around her hips, legs parted, and Dominic bent between them, his mouth on her sex.

Heat pooled between Sarah's own thighs as she watched, riveted. From her angle, she could see the movement of his mouth against Lily's blonde curls. First he'd cover her quim with his lips, then he'd draw back to flick his tongue over her jutting pink flesh, encouraging gasps from Lily, whose fingers gripped the edge of the table.

Sarah stepped back from the door, unable to look away, and jolted in alarm when hands closed over her arms.

"Are you enjoying watching?" Monsieur Cresson's voice asked in her ear.

She couldn't find the words to respond, so only nodded. She didn't turn away, and he didn't turn her away, instead crowding closer, his own breathing uneven, his palms sliding down her sleeves to her hands, then back up again to her shoulders.

Her breasts swelled in her bodice, and as if he sensed it, he glided his hands over them until she pushed against him. He chuckled, his mouth close to her throat, and slid his hand down to cover her mound through her skirts. She whimpered—the pressure was nice, but the touch not nearly intimate enough, not when she was watching Dominic's tongue dance over Lily's bare flesh, thrust into her pink opening. Sarah wanted Monsieur Cresson's fingers on her skin, and so reached for the hem of her skirt to lift it.

Beside her ear, he drew in a sharp breath, then assisted her with the heavy fabric, bunching it at her waist and sliding his hand between her parted legs, finding her slick flesh, stroking everywhere but where she wanted his touch most, making her swell with desire until she thought she would burst.

On the kitchen table, Lily climaxed, her body bowing,

her mouth open on a cry as Dominic licked and sucked, even after Lily eased back on the table, bonelessly.

Sarah wanted to experience the same sensation and swiveled her hips toward Monsieur Cresson's touch, but he danced his fingertips out of the way, frustrating her.

Arousing her.

Through the crack in the door, they watched Dominic rise and unfasten his trousers. He drew out his cock—not as handsome as Monsieur Cresson's. Sarah had never considered that cocks could appear different. He walked to the edge of the table and presented his erect manhood to Lily, who opened her eyes and smiled before rolling off the table and kneeling on the floor in front of him. Monsieur Cresson pressed his own hard sex—still clothed —against Sarah's bottom as Lily closed her hand around Dominic's and brought it to her mouth.

She dragged her tongue down the length of it, then back to toy with the tip, licking like she had a treat. Dominic groaned, and Lily eased her mouth down his shaft, taking the whole of him into her mouth. Sarah gasped at the sight and Monsieur Cresson bucked his hips against hers. Sarah remembered the strange urge to kiss him when he exposed his manhood to her. Was this why? Was this natural? She'd never heard of such a thing.

She watched her maid suck on the butler's cock as her artist played his fingers between her legs, teasing, spreading her wetness, before finally circling her swollen nub and bringing her to a climax that had her crying out, bracing her hand against the door and slamming it shut.

She had time to meet Dominic's startled gaze just before she did.

* * *

Sarah sat mortified in the hackney, unable to meet her maid's gaze. The tension between them was high with unasked questions.

"It doesn't matter to me that you watched us," Lily said at last. "How long were you there?"

"We watched him lick your sex until you cried out. And then we watched you take his cock in your mouth."

Lily gasped as if surprised to hear those words from her mistress. "Did you enjoy watching?"

A smile curved Sarah's lips despite herself. "Oh, quite. Was it as pleasurable as it seemed?"

"Oh, quite," Lily mimicked.

"Were you not embarrassed to have his mouth between your legs?"

"I prefer that to his cock."

What an odd thing to say, since Sarah's quim still ached to be filled by Monsieur Cresson's sex.

"I can show you what it feels like, if you wish, to have a tongue, a mouth, on your quim."

Sarah lifted her shocked gaze to Lily at that. The expression on the younger woman's face was unreadable. Surely she didn't mean—no. Besides, all Sarah wanted was Monsieur Cresson's mouth there, wanted to feel the surety of it. Of course he would know exactly what to do. And she would want to return the favor.

"Where did you learn—how to bring a man to pleasure with your mouth?"

It was Lily's turn to widen her eyes. "Do you wish to try that trick on your artist?"

Sarah's face heated.

"He's shown you things. Pleasure."

"He's cautious to leave me a virgin but I no longer care as much. I only want to know where these feelings lead."

"Because of him."

"It's wrong. I don't even know what he looks like but I can think of nothing else."

"Then I will show you."

CHAPTER 4

Sarah stood naked before her mirror that night, and watched her own hands glide over her body. She cupped her breasts as Monsieur Cresson had done, and pinched the nipples. A resulting pulse echoed between her thighs, which she parted, just a bit. Interesting how connected her body was. She circled her fingers around her nipples, and felt her arousal grow, throbbing, waiting for release. She glided a hand down her belly and stroked her curls, teasing herself with the possibility of touch, then stroked her breasts again. Would Monsieur Cresson's next portrait of her be a nude, holding her breasts? Would he touch her again? Would he put that great cock in her?

She should be more worried about her virginity, she knew, but her curiosity was a wild thing. What would it feel like to have his body joined with hers?

His cock was very much wider than her finger, than three of her fingers, but she parted her legs farther and slipped one finger into the part of her where he said his sex would go, the part of her that ached even when he was touching her clitoris.

Goodness, she was wet and swollen, but her caress felt good. She moved her finger deeper, because his cock was certainly longer than her finger. He would put the whole thing in her, would he not? She pushed deeper and wiggled her finger, and a small moan of pleasure escaped her lips. Yes, having him inside her would be delicious. Her clitoris, as he called it, begged for attention, so she slid her finger out of her body and across the quivering flesh. Yes. Yes. She didn't have the strength to resist, only flicked her fingers back and forth until the wave hit her, weakening her knees until she leaned forward against her dresser.

She looked up into the mirror and saw her flushed face and her own knowing eyes. Would Grayson Adams recognize her knowledge when they went riding tomorrow?

Was it wrong to dream about two different men helping her find her body's pleasure?

HER MOTHER HOVERED as Sarah welcomed Grayson Adams into the drawing room. She was surprised by her urge to look at his hands, to see their shape, to imagine how they'd feel against her skin. Her new discoveries of her body made her so aware of everything male about him, and how it would fit against everything female of her. Something flashed in his eyes, like curiosity, as he bent over her hand in greeting. Did he see the difference in her?

His scent wafted up and the familiarity of it took her aback. A moment passed before she recognized the scent.

He smelled like Monsieur Cresson's house, the oils, the paints, the turpentine. An idea struck her so hard, so quick, she wanted to shake it off. No, it couldn't be. Grayson Adams was not Monsieur Cresson. Why would he be? But the coincidence—Grayson paying attention to her as soon as she posed for the artist? Was it just coincidence?

Of course it was. Grayson didn't speak with an accent. And Monsieur Cresson surely didn't move about freely in society. Still, she couldn't shake the idea as he stepped back, sweeping his hand ahead of him.

"Shall we?"

He'd brought her a mare to ride, complete with sidesaddle. His man rode behind, a hat pulled low over his eyes, but he would serve as chaperone. Something about his posture drew her attention, until Grayson stepped up assist her into the saddle. Her gaze dropped to his hands, hoping to catch another hint, but he wore gloves. She allowed herself the pleasure of his hands encircling her waist as he lifted her, let her own hands rest on his broad shoulders, lingering there until she was settled in her seat. She'd forgotten how lovely his eyes were, a deep green, and she sought her memory for recollection of Monsieur Cresson's eyes when he wore his domino. They were light, she recalled, but it was hard to see in the candlelit room.

She made an effort to put her suspicions behind her as he mounted his own horse and they set out toward the park.

"The color of your habit suits you far better than the gowns you wear," he said, giving her another jolt. Had Monsieur Cresson not said something similar, that she needed to stay away from pastels? Her habit was a deep red, the one outfit she owned with real color.

"I thank you." She wished she could think of something to say. How easily she could speak to Monsieur Cresson. How much of that was because she was blindfolded, anonymous in a way? "Do you ride in the park often?"

"Not as much as I'd like. And never with such lovely company."

His flattery puzzled her. She knew she was not considered any great beauty by society, but Grayson seemed to have an unusual attraction for her.

"And you?" he asked. "Do you ride often in the park?"

"Not since my first season. I don't spend much time out of doors or in company, other than the balls and evening entertainments."

"I had noticed you keep to yourself much of the time, even there."

"I hardly have anything in common with the young girls coming out, and less with ladies my age who have married."

"You must be lonely."

She smiled, thinking of Monsieur Cresson—surely not the proper thing to do when riding out with a gentleman. "I manage to keep occupied."

Grayson kept the conversation going, asking her where she lived in the off-season, asking her social plans. For some reason, she heard the questions in an Italian accent and allowed herself to relax and enjoy herself.

Once they reached the park, she was aware of the attention they drew, the plain spinster and the dashing baron's son. She experienced the same freedom she felt in Monsieur Cresson's studio and allowed herself to revel in the attention.

She became brave enough to ask questions about his own life, in particular his travels, and her suspicions returned full-force when he mentioned a Grand Tour in Italy.

"Did you spend much time in any one place?" she asked, hoping not to alert him to the point of her questioning.

"I found Venice most intriguing. Rome was beautiful as well. So much art."

"And Florence? Did you go there?"

He glanced over at her and she bit her lower lip. Had she given herself away? Only Monsieur Cresson would be wary of answering, and if Grayson was not he, then he should not be aware.

"A few days. Is that a place you'd like to visit?"

"I love art," she said, hoping to prompt him to a similar comment.

He lifted a noncommittal shoulder and kept his attention straight ahead. "Italy is the place to visit."

"Perhaps I can convince my mother to travel there next season instead of here," Sarah said, hoping she hid her disappointment at being unable to draw out the truth. But of course he wouldn't tell her—he had too much to lose if anyone found out. That he couldn't trust her stung just a little. But really, how well did he know her?

Grayson returned her to her home an hour later and bent to kiss her hand before taking leave. "I'll see you at the Atherton ball tomorrow night?"

"Yes, I'll be there."

He straightened and gave her a smile that sent her most intimate places tingling, once again making her wonder if she was right about Grayson Adams's dual identity.

* * *

"TAKE OFF THE CHEMISE TODAY." Monsieur Cresson's voice was brusque as he walked into the studio after Sarah had obediently tied on the blindfold.

"You want me—unclothed?" she asked, turning toward him.

"Is that not what I said?"

She flinched at his sharp tone and hesitated, her hands fluttering near the hem of her chemise. "I've never been unclothed in front of any but my maid before."

"I know that. You are a virgin, are you not? I should

not expect that you would prance around naked in front of anyone."

Taking a deep breath, she removed the chemise, and faced him, feeling her nipples tighten in the cool air, feeling his gaze on her. She sensed he'd stopped all movement and stared at her.

"Is this how you want me?" She couldn't keep the taunt from her voice.

"Sit on the bed there," he said, his voice a growl. "I'll position you as I want you."

The idea of his hands on her, posing her, sent a shiver of longing through her. Would his fingers linger? Would he toy with her nipples, kiss her throat, pet her quim? Oh, how she longed for him to pet her.

She moved to the bed by feel and sat upon it. But his touch, when it came, was not gentle and caressing. No, it was businesslike as he parted her legs, wide, hooking her knees over each corner of the bed. His breathing changed and she wondered if he wanted to touch her as much as she wanted him to.

"Put your hands on your knees, and keep your back straight," he instructed.

She did as he asked, so her breasts pressed together between her arms, and then he gripped her chin, tilting it to the side and down. He reached up to loosen her hair and pushed it back over her shoulders, leaving her bare to him.

He said nothing as he dragged the chair across and sat with a creak of wood. She heard the scratch of his charcoal against the paper, heard him blow out a breath in frustration, rub out what he'd done and begin again. She wished she could watch him work, that he could trust her enough to let her see him. If he was in a better mood, she might tease him into letting her see. Instead, she wondered what irked him.

"Are you upset that I didn't come yesterday?" she asked at last.

He bit out a curse and she heard more rubbing. "No."

"You're very quiet today."

"This isn't working as I expected."

"Can I help?"

"No. Be quiet."

She pressed her lips together.

"Not like that. I want them parted, as if you know just what a man's thinking when he's looking at you, as if you can't wait for him to come to you and kiss you."

His voice rolled over her skin and her quim trembled. The way he drew in a breath told her he was aware of her arousal. He was always aware of her arousal.

"Did you have an enjoyable time?" he asked finally.

She had to stop herself from lifting her head in surprise. She hadn't told him she was going out for plea-sure—she merely told him she had an appointment. "I did."

"I didn't know you rode."

Her pulse throbbed in her throat. "You saw me? Did I see you?"

"Most definitely."

Her nipples tightened inexplicably at the knowledge

that he knew her outside of this room, that he could take what he knew of her outside of this room.

"Do you know Grayson Adams?"

"I do." Now humor laced his voice and fear sliced through her, cutting through her suspicion that they could be the same man. If they weren't, if they were only friends…

"You would never tell him what we do here." If they weren't the same man, had Grayson seen the sketches Monsieur Cresson had made? What would Grayson think if he knew she spread her legs, displayed her body for another man?

"I would not. You've put your trust in me."

"And yet you've not put your trust in me," she pointed out.

"Maybe soon. Do you like him?"

"Grayson? He's very charming. I admit to being surprised by his interest." She began to relax. She hadn't realized how accustomed she was to talking to him while he drew her.

"Why? Are you not as fascinating in the real world as you are here?"

His teasing tone made her blush. "Hardly, in either world."

"I find you so, and so must Grayson Adams." An idea occurred to her. "So may I ask him if he knows any Italian painters?"

Monsieur Cresson coughed. "He does not know me as such. Do not crease your brow."

He fell silent after that, leaving her mind to tumble

from one thought to another, falling back on something he'd said to her two days before.

"My maid informed me that the act we witnessed the other day was not so out of the ordinary, that men often drive a woman to pleasure with their mouths."

"Yes, and often women take a man's cock into their mouths, if they do not want intercourse."

"I cannot imagine a man wishing to perform such an act."

"It's very erotic, and it gives a woman great pleasure, more than his fingers would."

"Do you do it?"

"I have done so in the past."

"When you're drawing me, do you think about doing such a thing to me?"

"Yes, I imagine what your reaction would be if I did it to you."

"I want to know what it feels like."

"Usually it is foreplay, and a man puts his cock inside the woman afterwards, to relieve his own arousal. You are a virgin. I cannot take that liberty."

"You could put your cock in my mouth."

He blew out a chuckle. "You would not know what to do."

"Lily told me what to do."

He drew in a breath. "You discussed such a thing?"

"I wished to know." She parted her legs just a little wider, so wet she could feel the moisture on the insides of her thighs. "Please."

She sensed his movement, then he brushed his knuckles over her cheek.

"Then you will test what you learn on your Grayson? Will that not shock him?"

"I don't believe he will be as surprised as you think," she murmured, turning her face up until she could feel his breath on her lips.

His hand moved back to stroke through her hair, his fingers tangling in it a moment. "You are an uncommon woman."

She didn't have a chance to respond before he cupped his hand around the back of her head and covered her mouth with his. His lips were dry and warm before his tongue swept over her lower lip, sending sparks all along her body. He angled her head and his tongue probed her mouth for a moment before he straightened, his thumb still caressing her jaw. His ragged breathing dusted across her skin and for a moment she feared he'd walk away, but then his mouth was on hers again, harder, demanding, and his hands were on her skin, bringing her body closer so that the tips of her breasts rasped against the rough linen of his shirt. She whimpered, craving more contact, and he groaned, his hand sliding from where it caressed her bare spine to cup her breast, his thumb rubbing the tip. The ache between her parted legs intensified. No, just his mouth would not be enough to ease it, she was sure. She edged her hips closer to the edge of the bed and folded her legs about his. He made a sound in his throat as her naked quim pressed against the front of his trousers.

She could feel the hard ridge of his arousal beneath the fabric and tightened her legs to bring him closer.

He broke the kiss and brushed his lips along the edge of her jaw as he lowered her to the bed. He shifted his position so she could no longer rub against him. Instead, she felt his knee against the inside of her thigh, felt the heat of his body along hers as he braced himself over her. His mouth caressed her jaw before moving down to her throat and she gasped at the sensitivity of her skin, the roughness of his unshaven chin.

"Do you like that?" he asked, his fingers pulling at her nipple as he repeated the caress of her throat.

Pleasure zinged through her, making her mindless, and she arched her head back, offering him more. Every part of her was sensitive, aching, wanting. The wetness between her legs increased and she could smell her arousal in the air.

His mouth brushed her shoulder, then followed the slope of her breast. He hovered over her a moment, his breath hot against her skin and she lifted herself to him. He pulled back a little, then covered her breast with his mouth, hot, wet, pulling, and her quim twinged, wanting so much for him to fill her. Instead he suckled at her breast, as if he'd been able to think of nothing else, and she lost herself in the sensation until his fingertips traveled over her thigh. Another pulse of arousal slickened her sex, and then he was touching her, his fingers parting her curls, sliding along the sensitive flesh, teasing the place she wanted his cock before moving up to stroke over the swollen nub that craved his caress.

She recognized the prelude to her pleasure and pushed his hand away, though it took all her will-power to do so.

"Your mouth," she managed. "Your--"

She didn't complete the thought before he released her breast, spread her legs wider and dragged his tongue along the little nub. She bucked and cried out, but not with release, not yet. The tension in her body increased and he curved his hands under her bottom, lifting her, spreading her before parting his mouth over her sex, just as she'd dreamed. The tip of his tongue teased her opening before tracing the delicate folds and finding her clitoris, the little button she'd pressed the past two nights to bring herself to completion again and again.

He circled the flesh with his tongue, and she started to feel his fingertips at her opening, coasting back and forth over it when she wanted him to touch inside her as she had done. Then, as his tongue teased her button, his slick fingers caressed her rose.

Shame warred with pleasure as he stroked and probed, arousing nerve endings she hadn't realized she possessed. She moaned and pushed against his mouth, her climax sweeping through her as he continued to lick and stroke her.

As her body shuddered with the remains of the sensations, he lowered himself over her, his weight on her body delicious. He kissed her mouth gently, sweetly, then rested his head on her shoulder.

"You're the most incredible woman I know," he said, without the trace of an Italian accent.

CHAPTER 5

Grayson realized his mistake too late when Sarah whipped her head toward him, nearly striking his forehead with her chin.

"Grayson?" she demanded, and before he could stop her, she'd whipped off the blindfold and those dark brown eyes stared straight into his.

And then she smiled, a smile so bright and beautiful it took his breath away, before she rose over him, her hands on his shoulders as she leaned down to kiss him. He thought he heard her say, "I knew it," before she captured his mouth with hers.

Her kiss was untried but eager, and her hands coursed over his body as her tongue stroked his lips and inside his mouth. He curved his hands around her back, intending to push her away, to deal with the ramifications of her discovery, but she coursed her palm down the front of his shirt to close over his cock through his trousers.

"I thought about doing this all day yesterday," she said,

breaking the kiss to focus on unfastening his trousers, smoothing her palm over his erect sex before he could gather his thoughts to help her. "So different."

"From what?" he managed as she closed her fist around him, and he couldn't resist pumping against her hand. What did she mean she'd thought about doing this all day yesterday? That she knew? She couldn't possibly know. But the thought left his head as she squeezed.

"Lily had a dildo, but she showed me what to do, showed me where you were sensitive."

Just hearing the forbidden word on her lips made him nearly spill his seed. Instead, she lowered her mouth to brush over the head of him, her fist sliding up and down his length. He'd never had a woman know so much, and she learned from her maid, on a dildo. He watched as she opened her mouth around him, her hair spilling against his hips, and her tongue shyly touching the underside of his cock. When he sucked in his breath and arched his hips, she gained confidence, stroking more surely with her tongue and hand. She took a deep breath, and opened her mouth wider to take more of him into the hot cavern of her mouth, and Christ, it was all he could do not to grab the back of her head as he lifted his hips toward her and climaxed in her mouth.

She made a sound of surprise and started to back off before she stopped herself and closed her mouth around him, swallowing his seed.

His entire body tingled as she sat back on her knees, lips swollen and glistening, eyes dark with a womanly pleasure.

"I was given to understand it would take more effort on my part."

"If I hadn't been fantasizing about you for weeks, it might have." He looped his arm around her waist and drew her against his side. He knew he should talk about her discovery, but his brain hadn't reformed just yet. "A dildo? Your maid has a dildo?"

"I don't believe it's for her own pleasure. She said she doesn't care for cocks."

Would this woman ever stop surprising him? "Dominic seemed to believe she did."

"She said she did that so he wouldn't want to put his cock in her."

Grayson toyed with her hair. "You do know proper young ladies don't use such words. Or wonder about such acts."

"And proper young men don't paint such things. Or teach proper young ladies the correct terms."

"No one may know, Sarah," he said solemnly.

"Of course I understand. Whose reputation would suffer more, yours for painting or mine for posing?" She played with the opening of his shirt and slipped one of the buttons from its mooring, dipping her fingertips inside to play with his chest hair.

"I've maintained your anonymity in the paintings. No one will know. I need the same assurance from you."

She lifted startled eyes to his. "Of course I will keep your secret. We both have much to lose."

"You don't seem too concerned about your reputation."

She drew in a sharp breath and sat up. "I served your purpose, then," she said stiffly, reaching for her discarded chemise.

"You came to me," he reminded her, turning on his side toward her. "You did everything I asked of you. I wonder how eager you are to shock your mother by revealing what you've done here."

She whirled on him. "Is that what you think I am? A rebellious girl?"

He motioned to the sketches, wondering at his need to push her away. He'd already gotten too close, risked too much, revealed too much. Did he risk her retribution by pursuing this argument? The thought came a second after he said, "I have evidence in front of me."

For a moment she was perfectly still, then she started trembling all over and tears filled her eyes. His heart tugged and he sat up to reach for her but she'd turned away to dress. He let his hand fall to his side on the bed, feeling the warmth from her body, wanting her back in his arms and unsure how to get her there, now that he'd so effectively chased her off. Instead, he watched her dress, and not even completely at that, before she fled.

THE CHANCES of getting into the house without her mother seeing her were slim. Sarah's hair was hastily pinned up by Lily in Grayson's kitchen, her eyes were red-rimmed from the tears she'd shed on her way home, and she had left her stockings behind in her haste. No, she did not want her mother to see her like this.

"Just tell her you are unwell," Lily suggested when Sarah hesitated on the doorstep. Lily had not asked one question about Sarah's distress, but she knew her mother would, unwell or not.

"Perhaps you can distract her while I slip upstairs," Sarah said hopefully.

"Not if she does not want to be distracted," Lily replied.

That was true. "At least draw her away from the entrance so I can slip upstairs and straighten up before she sees me. How am I going to get myself together for the ball tonight?"

"Tell your mother you are unwell," Lily repeated.

"Grayson might be there." Was she some kind of glutton, wanting to see a man who had no emotion for her?

"What happened back there?"

Sarah shook her head, not trusting herself to speak.

"All right, I'll find your mother. I'll be upstairs in a bit to help you."

Sarah shook her head again. "I don't want—I just need to be alone and think."

"Did he make love to you?"

She shook her head again. "No. No. I wanted him to, and he turned it against me. I just—I need to be alone. Please. Go. Find my mother."

Sarah waited a moment after Lily ducked into the house, then hurried for the stairs, not looking left or right, just needing to get—

"Sarah, are you all right?" her mother's voice called from the parlor.

Sarah froze halfway up the stairs, wishing she knew swear words to mutter under her breath. She smoothed her hands over the front of her dress, then her hair, and willed tears from her eyes before she turned toward the parlor.

Where her mother sat with Mrs. Sawyer and her daughter Juliet. Lovely.

Sarah forced a smile and moved back down the stairs to stop in the doorway. "Good afternoon."

"Please come join us," her mother said, with a touch of steel beneath the gentle request.

"I'm not feeling quite the thing, Mother. I need to go lie down."

Her mother rose and inspected her critically. *Please, please don't let her see the truth.*

"You do look ill, Sarah. Were you not dressed warmly enough today?"

The question almost surprised a giggle out of her. She had been completely undressed not an hour before. "That must be it. I've caught a chill. I would not wish for anyone else to suffer, so I must excuse myself. Mrs. Sawyer, Juliet, please forgive me."

She stood on shaking legs waiting for her mother's permission to take her leave. Finally her mother nodded and she turned and fled, never so grateful in her life to be alone.

* * *

SHE KNEW her mother would check on her as soon as her company left, so she undressed quickly, bathed in the warm bowl of water Lily brought her, ignoring the girl's curious expression, put on her nightclothes and crawled into bed. She wanted to give into the tears clogging her throat but didn't want to risk the need to explain them to her mother.

Why was she giving this man this power over her? She had made her choice, and she never expected him to judge her on it, but of course he would. He would judge her decision and her curiosity and her willingness to do things no unmarried woman would know about. Everyone would judge her if they knew. But his judgment felt like a betrayal.

As expected, her mother knocked on the door a short time later and walked in without waiting for an invitation. Sarah remained in bed in the darkened room, but her mother would have none of that. Instead she walked to the windows and pushed open the curtains before approaching the bed and touching Sarah's head with her palm.

"You are not warm. Are you sure you have chills?"

"I cannot seem to get warm, and I have a headache." From holding back her tears, but her mother didn't need to know that.

"I suppose this is a way to get out of going to the Locke's ball tonight?"

"I do not mind going to the ball. If I rest, perhaps I'll feel more up to it."

Her mother regarded her for a moment. "There is more you aren't telling me."

"No. There isn't."

Her mother hesitated, then said, "I'll send Lily up with some soup, and will check back in a few hours."

She nodded gratefully and closed her eyes before her mother closed the door.

* * *

SARAH'S HEADACHE lingered as she stood at the edge of the dance floor, but she was too anxious to see Grayson again to use her headache as an excuse to stay home. She scanned the crowd to no avail. He hadn't come. He wouldn't come—why would he? And she was a fool, the worst kind of fool for putting her hopes, her beliefs in a man.

But hiding in her room would give him too much power. So she danced and smiled and for some reason she attracted more partners than usual. Her mother was happy, so Sarah pretended to be happy, and for a little while, she forgot all about Grayson Adams.

But when she went home she cried herself to sleep.

* * *

"YOU'RE NOT GOING OUT ANYMORE," her mother commented over breakfast a few days later.

"I'm still not feeling quite myself."

"Who broke your heart?"

Sarah snapped her gaze to her mother's. "No one. Of course, no one."

"Grayson Adams."

"No."

"He asked to be introduced, he took you riding, and nothing else? What happened on the ride?"

"Apparently I didn't charm him enough."

"And everyone saw you together. Everyone is asking why he hasn't been to any of the balls since, as if I would know. But whatever it was didn't happen on the ride, it happened the day after. When you came home upset."

"No, this has nothing to do with Grayson Adams."

Her mother sat back, lips pressed together. "I know a broken heart when I see it."

"No. I didn't even know him well enough to let him break my heart."

"Miss Dusenberry," the maid interrupted, walking into the breakfast room carrying a large box. "This just came for you."

Sarah was on her feet before she could think. "What is it?"

"It's from Madame Ariana's Modiste."

Sarah frowned. "I haven't ordered anything from her in months."

"Perhaps you've forgotten. Open it. I want to see," her mother said as Sarah took the box and placed it on the end of the table.

Sarah didn't need encouragement. She tugged at the ribbon holding the box closed and opened the box with reverence to reveal a deep blue evening gown in the finest silk, trimmed with embroidered ribbon instead of the lace that usually trimmed her dresses, leaving this one with a sleek, elegant look. She smoothed her hands over the fabric before lifting it by the shoulders to see that instead of puffy sleeves, these were fitted to the elbow to flare in a fall-away style.

"Why would you order such a color? That is not in fashion at all," her mother said, rising to stand beside her.

"I didn't," Sarah breathed, knowing before she opened the enclosed card.

I'll see you Friday. MC.

Her heart skipped a beat, then she gathered the dress and hurried upstairs to try it on. Lily followed to help.

The dress fit like a dream, molding to her body, not needing all the petticoats that were usually in fashion. In fact it skimmed over her hips and belly, all one piece instead of the separate bodice that was the current style.

"How did he know my size?" she asked Lily as she stared at her reflection in the mirror.

"Dominic asked me to tell him."

"So you knew."

"I didn't know it would be something so unique. It will certainly stand out."

Sarah paused and drew her lower lip between her teeth. "I wish I didn't have to wait until Friday to wear it."

Lily's eyebrows went up. "I know where you can wear it tonight, if you can slip away from your mother. Monsieur Cresson has an art show tonight."

CHAPTER 6

Sarah shivered outside of the art gallery and pulled her wrap tighter about herself, though the temperature was mild. Her nerves were on edge. She had pled a headache and said she was going to bed, only to dress and slip out with Lily's help. The maid had a hackney waiting at the corner and Sarah had run to it. Now she stood in front of the gallery and wondered what she'd done.

She lifted her chin. She'd come this far. She wasn't running away now.

She mounted the steps into the gallery, wishing for once that she had a friend, someone she could have trusted to come with her.

She was unprepared to see so many familiar faces as she entered the gallery. She hadn't realized so many high society people would be here. Her mother would certainly hear about this tomorrow. She stiffened in anticipation of what her punishment would be.

She smiled and scanned the room for Grayson, her attention caught by the paintings on the wall, all done in soft colors. She could understand how he managed to display them—the details, while precise, were not obvious. She stopped in front of one done in blues and lavenders, an amazingly erotic painting, so finely detailed, and she felt a blush stain her cheeks.

Grayson pivoted when he heard the murmurs and saw the blue silk that he'd paid a small fortune for sweep into the room and around the corner.

What was she thinking, coming here? His fear was not that she'd expose him, but that she would be exposed to scandal. The people who attended his art show were married people, and a young unmarried woman, unaccompanied, was out of place. Especially a young unmarried woman staring at the painting of her own quim.

He glanced around the room and didn't see Dominic, so he excused himself from the gentlemen he'd been in conversation with and crossed the room toward her. She turned, her eyes widening when she saw him. He took her hand and swept in a bow over it, bringing it to his lips.

"I'm so pleased you could meet me," he said, his voice low. "You look lovely, Miss Dusenberry."

He straightened and looked into her eyes. She returned his gaze steadily, even lifting her brows as if daring him to say anything to expose her. Clearly she didn't believe he was the one who should be wary. He tightened his hand around her upper arm and guided her away from the crowd.

"What are you doing here?" he asked.

"I wanted to thank you for the gown. I had no idea there would be quite so many people I know," she said, glancing around.

"You look stunning, but Sarah, this is not the place for you."

"Why not? No one knows who you are, or what they're looking at, for that matter."

"You don't know that. And it doesn't matter. You come here alone, and you stand out, Sarah." His lips tightened. "At least people have seen us together. They may doubt my judgment bringing you here, but there is that."

"You have an amazing turnout," she said when she sensed him relax. "Are these all the paintings?"

"No. I've not finished all of them, and there are some I dare not display. Not here."

"This is very exciting. I had no idea you had so many. Do you sell them?"

"Yes, but usually not here. I make most of my sales overseas." He offered her a glass of champagne and let his gaze travel over her. "The color suits you. I would have preferred red, but Madame Amaria pointed out it is not the color for a young woman of breeding."

She smiled. "I imagine."

He lifted his hand to her hair, let it fall after caressing a tendril that hovered near her cheek. "I'm sorry for the things I said. The dress—was an apology."

"Not an invitation."

A dimple creased his cheek. Her heart fluttered. She hadn't noticed that feature before. "The invitation was for Friday, not tonight. How did you know I was here?"

"Lily told me."

"Ah." He trailed his fingers down her sleeve. "I've missed you, Sarah." He closed his fingers around hers. "Let's go."

She smiled, enjoying the freedom of looking into his eyes and seeing both of the men she knew. "Don't you need to be here?" She inclined her head toward the wall behind her.

"They don't know who I am, remember?" He tucked her hand into the crook of his arm and led her toward the door.

Three men entered the room at that time, looking about at the walls, then scanning the guests, who quieted as they turned.

"Mr. Adams?" one man asked, stepping forward to stand in front of Grayson.

"Yes? And you are?"

"Inspector Payton. You need to come with me, sir."

"Inspector? Why?"

Another perusal of the walls, then judgmental eyes turned back to Grayson. "Indecent displays. Would you really like for me to arrest you in front of your friends?"

Grayson stepped away from Sarah, dropping her hand. She froze in shock. He gave her a regretful look, then nodded to the inspector and accompanied him out the door, leaving her alone and wondering what had just happened before she was herded out with the others.

* * *

GRAYSON WALKED out of the magistrate's office and down the steps a different man. He didn't want to think about returning to his studio, seeing the emptiness there after his paintings had been confiscated. All his work, the paintings of Sarah…he didn't have the heart to recreate them, even if he could. The emotions that had been present in the room when he'd drawn her could not be duplicated.

"Sir!"

He looked up to see Dominic beckon him from the side of a carriage parked along the street. Relief quivered in his muscles. Soon he would be alone where he could brood in private. He nodded at his man and stepped into the carriage to find he was not alone.

Sarah sat on one bench, her reticule dangling from her wrist, still wearing the gown he'd bought her when he'd been arrogant and foolish, invincible.

Now his reputation was in tatters and she was here at the magistrates—why?

"Sarah, you shouldn't be here," he said wearily, heaving himself onto the seat across from her.

"I came to get you."

He snapped his head up. So that was why he hadn't been asked for coin, had just been released. "Sarah. You didn't--"

"Your fine is paid." She lifted her chin stubbornly.

Christ she had beautiful eyes. He'd made her hide them for weeks, and now they shone with an emotion he didn't want to identify. "Why?" he asked brusquely.

She folded her hands primly in her lap. "Because you needed help."

"Not from you."

Her eyebrows arched. "Why not?"

Little fool, she had to know the answer. "Because my reputation is destroyed and yours will be as well if anyone associates you with me." He let that sink in a moment before his curiosity got the better of him. "Where did you get the money?" She'd come to pose for him for the money to travel, after all.

Even in the dim light inside the carriage, he saw the blush tinge her cheeks. "I took it from the household funds. I am assured you can replace it before my mother notices it's missing."

The last was said as something of a question. Shock rolled through him. "You stole from your mother?"

"I borrowed," she said, stressing the word.

"Why?"

"I didn't want you to spend any longer than you had to in that place."

"I have been taking care of myself for some time now." He couldn't resist softening toward her, after the chance she took for him.

"I understand."

"I thank you." He reached across the carriage and took her gloved hand in his. "But you should not risk so much for me." He wasn't worth it.

She lifted those beautiful eyes to his and he saw something in there that frightened him more than the concern for his paintings, for his reputation. Christ, was the girl in love with him?

"I'll take you to my home and get you the money to replace your mother's funds, then you need to be on your way."

She nodded, her fingers tightening on her purse.

He'd wanted to go by his apartment first, to see what paintings remained from the raid, but the longer he spent in Sarah's company, the more dangerous for both of them, a danger that went far beyond his reputation.

The carriage pulled alongside his townhouse and Grayson was out of his seat before the conveyance swayed to a stop. "Wait here. I'll bring the money to you. What was the sum?"

She shifted forward on her seat as if to follow, but one look from him had her shrinking back. She told him the sum and he slammed the door decidedly.

He had not gone five steps in his house when he heard the swish of skirts behind him. He pivoted to see Sarah in the entryway, hands clasped over her purse, appearing undecided for just a moment before determination brightened her features and she crossed the floor toward him. She curved her hand around the back of his head and brought his mouth down to hers. He stiffened for a moment, but the sweetness of her mouth, the generosity of her gesture melted his resolve to keep away from her. He curved his hands around her waist and parted his lips for the tentative foray of her tongue.

The pure innocence in her kiss should have had him shoving her out the door, coin in hand. Instead, it enflamed him and he brought her closer, encouraging her inexperienced caresses. His cock grew heavy as her fingers curled through his hair, stroked the back of his neck, as her breasts rubbed against his chest.

Virgin, he reminded himself, even as his hands slid up to cup her breasts through the silk of her dress. No corset here, only firm breasts, tight nipples, and he swirled his thumbs over the sensitive tips, causing her to gasp into his mouth. He took over the kiss then, tasting her lips, her tongue, sliding along it in the rhythm he craved.

She whimpered and broke the kiss and for a moment he thought she'd bolt. Instead, she pressed her body closer to his and angled her head back, inviting his kisses on her long white throat. He obliged, running his lips up and down the line of soft skin until she shuddered, clutching his arms. He trailed his lips across her exposed collarbone to the hollow of her throat, and felt her breathing grow faster, tempting him to brush his lips across the tops of her breasts. She released her grip on his arms to tangle her fingers in his hair, guiding him downward. He allowed himself just a taste of the skin between her breasts before he stepped back, breaking contact.

She stared up at him, eyes, wide, dark with desire, breasts lifting with each breath, nipples peaked against the silk of her dress. He could smell her arousal, and his own was excruciating.

But he wouldn't take a virgin in the entryway of his home. He shouldn't take a virgin at all, but a man with his disposition had only so much strength.

She's in love with you, the voice in his head warned. *If you take her virginity, you owe her more than an affair.*

He knew that. He *knew* that. He was no cad to deflower a virgin and cast her aside. After all, hadn't he been the man pursuing her, sending her the dress, attending balls he knew she'd attend? She'd fascinated him for weeks. Was it love? He didn't know—he'd never experienced love. When he'd bought the dress, he'd had every intention of courting her, but that had been when his reputation was intact. Now, did he want to risk bringing her down with him?

"I'm not the man for you," he said, those words the hardest he'd ever had to say.

"You are the only man for me," she countered, taking a step toward him.

He stepped back. "My reputation—society will no longer embrace me, Sarah."

"You believe that's important to me? Does it embrace me now?"

"It welcomes you. It may not be important now, but in time--"

"In time I don't wish to be here. I want to be in Europe or the Americas, somewhere, anywhere, I can experience life. And I want you to show me." She reached behind her head to unfasten the dress, her fingers fumbling with the buttons. He watched helplessly as the fabric loosened around her shoulders and she shrugged to let it fall to her waist, like the most experienced courtesan. Her breasts thrust, full and firm, against the silk of her chemise. His hands itched to feel the weight and texture, his mouth longed to close over a dark nub and draw it into his mouth.

She kept her gaze steady on him and waited. With a growl, he crossed to her, swept her into his arms and carried her up the stairs to his bedroom.

* * *

SARAH QUIVERED with anticipation as Grayson sat her on her feet in a bedroom decorated in dark colors and dominated by a massive bed. He coursed his hands down her back and made short work of the blue dress, which pooled at her feet. He bent to sweep it up and folded it over a chair as she stood awkwardly in the middle of the room, uncertain what to do next.

He turned to face her, tugging off his jacket and placing it over her dress before he returned to take her in his arms, his hand curving under her jaw to lift her mouth to his.

His kiss was warm and thorough, his tongue teasing, then sliding deep, filling her with the taste of him, making her whole body heat. His cock pushed against her belly, his fingers toyed with the tip of her breast. She unbuttoned his shirt and spread the fabric open over his broad chest. Her fingers danced over the defined muscles, glided down his belly until he drew in a sharp breath and grabbed her hand.

She pulled free and eased toward the bed, knowing what to do now, drawing the chemise over her head and tossing it aside. His gaze riveted to her as he shrugged out of his shirt and unfastened his pants, his sex jutting toward her. For a moment she thought about going down on her knees and taking him in her mouth again. She could feel the texture of his skin against her tongue, could taste his musky essence. But before she could act, he was beside her, having removed his boots, but still wearing his breeches.

She didn't hesitate, and closed her hand around his erection, eliciting a groan from him as she slid her fingers up and down his length. It was unnerving, actually, knowing what to do but not what to expect. He shucked off his pants and closed his hands over her shoulders to ease her back onto the bed. The duvet beneath her was soft and she sank into it, for a moment thinking she'd fallen down a rabbit hole.

Then he was over her, braced on his elbow, toying with her hair, his other hand sliding over her hip and between her parted legs.

She bowed toward him at the first brush of his fingers over her damp curls, and he delved deeper, to tease her opening before sliding up to toy with the little nub of pleasure, swollen now with anticipation. He bent his head to swallow her gasp as he circled and stroked it before dipping back into her body, stretching, pushing deeper than she'd had the courage to do. The sensation was at once alien and delicious, and she moved against his hand, wanting to follow the sensations, but also wanting to hold back, to feel the full experience of desire when his body entered hers.

"Soon," he murmured to her whimpered pleas. "I want you ready."

Another finger joined the first, stretching her, causing a twinge of discomfort before he began sliding them up and down, in and out, in much the same way he'd pushed his cock in her mouth. The rhythm of fucking.

Anxiety tightened her stomach. His cock was much wider and longer than his two fingers. Would it hurt? Was all the pleasure to be had on the outside of her body? Why did her quim long to be filled?

Grayson released her mouth and dipped his head to sip her nipple between his lips, drawing on it, and she no longer cared about the possibility of pain, only wanted his sex inside her, showing her what pleasure he could. She threaded her fingers through his hair, holding him to her breast, parting her legs wider. He rewarded her by sweeping his thumb over the little button of pleasure, and she pushed against his hand, taking now three fingers deeper into her. He rubbed his cock against her thigh and she shifted toward it.

"Please, Grayson. Please."

He lifted his head from her breast and removed his touch from between her legs as he moved over her, kneeling between her legs, the rough hair of his thighs brushing against the tender insides of hers. She held her breath as he positioned the broad head of his cock against her entrance, then he swept her hair back from her face as he pressed forward, stretching her, filling her, and once the pinch of discomfort eased, stroking against sensitive spots she didn't know she had.

"Sarah?" he asked, his voice strangled as he looked into her eyes.

She realized then that she wasn't breathing and quickly took a breath before nodding and tightening her legs about his hips, pushing hers into his, testing his depth, his breadth. His breath hitched and he drew back slowly, the drag of his erection along her inner walls exquisite pleasure. Her muscles clenched, holding him inside, and he slid deeper, the hair at the base of his cock pressing against her tender folds. He rolled against her, so deep inside her body he took her breath away. She tightened her grip on his shoulders and looked up into his green eyes, saw the patience, the desire as he moved over her, in her.

Then he lowered his mouth to her neck, to her collarbone, his soft lips and beginning of his beard such a jarring contrast, and her skin was so tender, each rasp sent another pulse of arousal to her sex, tightening her around him, making her slicker. He coursed down the slope of one breast to take her nipple into his mouth, his tongue rubbing, lips drawing. She arched toward him, wanting more. He closed his teeth over the tip and she gasped, gliding her hands down his back to hold him closer. He released her breast and rose over her again, his strokes increasing in speed, pushing deeper and deeper into her. The intensity of the pleasure increased, but like before, something was missing. She wanted to climax, and the way his cock filled her—and seemed to grow inside her—was exciting, and felt so good. The way he kissed her skin felt so good. The way his sweat-slickened skin rubbed over hers felt so good. But maybe there was something she was supposed to be doing to bring about her own completion.

As if he sensed her frustration, Grayson rose on his knees, his hands cupped around her bottom, parting her legs wider as he plunged into her. His gaze flicked from her face to her spread legs.

She cried out as her body tightened around him, but she needed something she didn't know how to ask for.

"I'm watching my cock move in and out of you," he murmured, as if he knew she needed something more. "Christ, you're so wet and hot and tight around me, squeezing me." His fingers clenched her bottom as if to show her. "Does it feel good to you?"

"Touch me," she gasped in desperation. "Grayson, touch me."

He stopped thrusting and studied her a moment. Heat crawled up her skin. Had she done something wrong? But then a grin split his face and he dragged his hands around to tease the crease between her hips and thighs, making her sex swell. Then he stroked his thumb over the swollen nub as he pumped slowly, watching her face as he teased her, ramming his full length into her and circling his cock as he circled his fingers.

Tension made her muscles tremble, tighten, before she flew apart in a million pieces, melting against his hand, crying out in a voice she didn't recognize as he drained the last bit of pleasure from her, his body plunging into hers until he stilled above her, his seed pulsing into her.

Then his hand was on her face, his fingers smelling of

her. He stroked her cheek, her lower lip, and covered her mouth with his in the most tender of kisses, his lips soft and reverent as they moved over hers. She let her eyes drift shut as his fingertips traced her face, and then he slid free.

He ended the kiss and lay beside her, his arm looped around her waist. Curiosity getting the better of her, she opened her eyes. His eyes were closed, dark lashes fanning over his cheeks, his lips parted, his hair damp around his temples and forehead. His shoulders and chest were slick, too, and well-muscled, so beautifully defined in the light from the fireplace that she couldn't resist tracing them, her fingers skimming over his skin and eliciting an indrawn breath. His stomach was flat with a line of soft hair descending from his navel to flare out around his cock, which now rested against his thigh, no less fascinating in a flaccid state.

He captured her wrist before she could explore further. "A few moments, if you please."

She lifted her gaze to his. He smiled and threaded his fingers through her hair.

"Was it not everything you expected?"

"It was, and more." She only wished she had the words to describe how—complete she felt at this moment.

"You look stunning just now," he said, then tensed suddenly and rolled away. "I must draw you."

She blinked and lifted her head from the pillow. "Now? But--"

He hushed her and drew a sketchpad from beside the

nightstand, opening the top drawer to retrieve charcoal. "Stay as you are."

Grayson sat in a nearby chair and propped the pad on his naked lap, first tracing the outline of her body as she reclined on his bed, wanting to capture her replete pose, wanting to show the effects of a woman well-loved, the marks of his mouth on her body, her swollen mouth, dreamy eyes. She watched him as he drew her, and his cock began to swell again, as if aware he was touching her remotely, through the charcoal and paper. He should send her home, not fuck her again, but he had to, could already feel her sex squeezing him, welcoming him, milking him.

He forced himself to put the finishing touches on her face before he set the pad aside and rose to return to the bed, fully erect. He half-expected she would recoil or be frightened. Instead, delight lit her eyes and she pushed to a sitting position to reach for him. He let himself enjoy her delicate caress before removing her touch and kneeling on the bed beside her. She stretched out on her back, spreading her legs in welcome. He bent to kiss her, the head of his cock rubbing her inner thigh before he pressed it against her quim, but he didn't enter her.

"Do you trust me?" he asked against her mouth.

"Of course."

"Get on your knees and place your hands on the headboard."

Her eyes widened, but when he straightened to give her room, she did what he asked, presenting him with curvy white buttocks. He smoothed his palms over them as he knelt behind her, between her parted legs, and lowered his mouth to her shoulder, eliciting a gasp from her. He smiled against her skin and coasted his hands up her waist to cup her full breasts, toying with her nipples as he nudged at the crevice of her buttocks with his cock. She opened herself wider and shifted to invite him inside, but he denied himself a moment longer, trailing his hand over her flat belly to pet her soft sex, slick with fresh desire. He teased her swollen clitoris with a few strokes, until she moved into his touch, and then he removed it, settling his hands on her hips again. He angled her forward just a bit, making her vulnerable, and slid home, his groin grinding against her buttocks, his length swallowed in her hot wet channel.

"Christ," he muttered against her shoulder when her muscles tightened around him, when he felt the vibration of her moan all along his body. "Am I hurting you?"

"No." Her voice was pitched lower than usual. "No. Please."

"Please what?" He rubbed his mouth across the line of her shoulder.

"Move. I need to feel you move in me."

He clenched his teeth as he fought for control against the desire her words elicited. "I'll show you, and you move with me. Yes?"

She nodded her head frantically, her hair falling forward. "Yes."

He drew out of her, then, guiding her hips, pulled her toward him as he slid deep again, showing her the rhythm. She was a quick learner, and when she rocked against him with confidence, he released her hips to stroke her breasts, plucking the nipples, wishing he could reach them with his mouth. But he loved the sight of his cock plunging into her this way, loved feeling the curve of her buttocks against his groin, loved the freedom to touch her and make her wild.

He glided his palm down her belly to play with her clitoris through the curls, not a direct caress, but one that had her rolling her hips, at once wanting his touch on her swollen button, and his cock fully seated inside her. It made for an exquisite sensation along his sex, and her channel grew slicker, her breathing more ragged. His own control was held by the thinnest of threads as her tight little quim moved up and down his length, gripping him like a slick fist. He parted her folds with his fingertip, letting her ride it as he pinned her body against his, his cock buried deep in her as she wriggled against his finger seeking her pleasure.

She found it with an expulsion of breath and a quiver of muscles, and with his finger still on her clitoris, he pushed her forward and slammed his hips into her, driving deeper and deeper into her pulsing flesh before his balls tightened and the orgasm ripped out of him, taking part of his soul with it.

He dropped over her back, panting, his muscles no longer able to follow his commands. He managed to curl a hand around her waist and pulled her down to the bed beside him, nestled in the curve of his body. He was aware of her heavy breathing before he fell asleep.

* * *

Sarah stood in the entryway of her home, her reticule clutched in front of her, her mother on the stairs in front of her as dawn's light illuminated the disappointment in her mother's face.

"What have you done, Sarah?"

"I've—decided to make my own choices. I've—decided I don't care to be part of English society."

"And you won't be if anyone saw you walk in at this hour. Do you have any idea of the damage you have done? Not only to your reputation, but—you'll never marry now. No man wants another's leavings."

"Mother, I was never going to marry in any case. I'm one and twenty, much too old for any man to want me. Until tonight."

"But he didn't propose."

Sarah's face heated. "No."

"Only flipped up your skirts."

So much more than that.

"I need to send you out of town before everyone discovers what you've done. It will be irregular to leave in the middle of the Season, but we can claim illness or some such. We can stay in the country for the rest of the year, and hopefully by next year everyone will have forgotten. Unless he's planted a child in your belly."

Sarah planted her feet. "I don't want another season. I don't want another year in society, another moment. But I don't want to go home. I want to go to Italy." Even if it meant being away from Grayson.

Her mother gaped. "What?"

"I want to travel in Europe, see the world. I want to know more than England."

"I despise Europe. You know that."

"Then let me go alone."

"After what you just did? How can I ever trust you? And if you refuse to marry, your behavior will reflect on me."

"Then hire a chaperone."

"So you can slip away from her as well, do whatever you have a mind to do? No, we're going back to Cumbria." She turned to go up the stairs.

"No." Sarah didn't know where the word came from, but she would die before she'd go back to the isolation of their country home in the Lake District. Beautiful, yes, but lonely, and so much more restrictive than even London. "No, I'll go to Europe, but I'm not going home."

Her mother pivoted and stared. "Who are you? I don't even recognize you."

"Because you don't look." Sarah took a step up toward her mother. "Please, Mother. If you must send me away, send me someplace I can be happy, not someplace to punish me."

Anger tightened her mother's features, then sorrow softened them. "I wanted so much more for you."

"But you never asked me what I wanted, and I never could tell you because I didn't want to disappoint you. Now I know what I've done. I'm content with my choices. But I want to make my own now. Please."

* * *

SARAH STEPPED off the train onto the platform in Paris. She had hardly blinked on the ride from the coast to the city, but now that they'd arrived in the city, she couldn't stop staring. Even the glass and stone station was more exotic than anything in England. Her chaperone, Miss Worthington, called to her as she moved along the platform, taking in the sights, absorbing them as if they restored her broken heart.

She hadn't heard from Grayson after their night together, but to be fair, she hadn't contacted him, either, until the last minute when she sent Lily with word that she'd be leaving town for France, on her way to Italy. Perhaps, though, she'd discounted Paris as a destination. Perhaps she could stay here a little longer than planned. She moved through the crowd and into the building, following the architecture with her eyes, and not even realizing she was drifting until she bumped into someone. Firm hands clasped her upper arms.

"I'm so sorry," she said, placing her hand over her hat to hold it in place as she turned to the person she'd collided with.

And looked into familiar green eyes, crinkled in a smile. Her heart lurched.

"Grayson."

"I've been waiting for you for three days."

She blinked. "We were delayed—weather over the channel. You've been waiting for me?"

"Do you think I could let you walk away? Have I not told you that you're the most incredible woman I've ever known?"

She took a step back, breaking his hold on her. "You—I didn't think—"

"You didn't believe me."

"No."

He stroked his knuckles down her cheek. "I don't lie, Sarah. I hide things, but I don't lie." He moved back as well, giving her breathing room. "You left without saying good-bye."

"I didn't know—I wasn't sure how. I only sent word because I didn't want you to worry."

"And I appreciate it." He glanced past her. "Are you traveling alone?"

"I have a chaperone." She waved her hand in the direction of the doors.

"And you'll be seeing the sights with her?"

"She's very grateful for it."

"Then I'll be sorry to disappoint her. I wish to be the one to introduce you to the beauty of Europe."

Her pulse quickened. "Yes?"

"But I rather think we should do it in the manner of our countrymen, don't you, and see it as a wedding trip?"

She stared. "A wedding--?"

"I have a friend, a minister, who will be happy to perform the ceremony on the morrow." He captured her hand and brought it to his lips. "Miss Dusenberry, will you consent to be my bride?"

She felt her face heat and she sought the words. "I'm not increasing," she managed at last.

He cocked his head curiously. "Should that matter?"

"I don't want you to believe you must wed me because you bed me."

The grin encompassed his face now and he moved closer. "Miss Dusenberry, I must say you are quite the poetess, but the thought did not cross my mind. I want you, by my side, in my bed, until the end of time. And to that end, I'll go the traditional route and face the minister. What do you say? Will you be traditional with me?"

Everything in her thrilled as she looked into those beloved green eyes, as she thought of the new future that rolled out before them. She returned his smile and dipped her head coquettishly.

"Only this once."

ABOUT THE AUTHOR

Emma Jay has been writing longer than she'd care to admit, using her endless string of celebrity crushes as inspiration for her heroes. Emma, married 35 years (wed at the age of 8, of course) believes writing romance is like falling in love, over and over again. Creating characters and love stories is an addiction she has no intention of breaking.

Her Perfect Getaway

Her Island Fantasy

Her Moonlit Gamble

Blackwolf Hot Shot series

All on the Line

Crossing the Line

Standing on the Line

Standalones

Riding Out the Storm

Two Step Temptation

Show Off

Off Limits

Lessons for Teacher

Two Nights on the Island

Hot and Bothered

www.ingramcontent.com/pod-product-compliance
Lightning Source LLC
Chambersburg PA
CBHW051233160726
47994CB00002B/867